Penny Post Boy

Stories linking with the History
National Curriculum Key Stage 2.

First published in 1999 by Franklin Watts
96 Leonard Street, London EC2A 4XD

Editor: Claire Berridge
Designer: Jason Anscomb
Consultant: Dr Anne Millard, BA Hons, Dip Ed, PhD

A CIP catalogue record for this book
is available from the British Library.

ISBN 0 7496 3362 X (hbk)
    0 7496 3544 4 (pbk)

Dewey Classification 383/941.081

Printed in Great Britain

Penny Post Boy

by **Karen Wallace**

Illustrations by Greg Gormley

W

FRANKLIN WATTS

NEW YORK • LONDON • SYDNEY

1

A Penny for Luck!

Sam Chumley stood in the front parlour and stared into the square sideboard mirror. The room he knew so well was reflected around him. Two little tables with lace tablecloths sat on either side of his mother's armchair. A huge green potted plant that was his grandmother's pride and joy stood in a corner. Above a big dark wooden table was a painting of Sam as young boy, in a sailor suit, on his first trip to the beach.

Sam squared his shoulders and stared into the middle of the glass.

A young man in a uniform with shiny buttons stared back at him. Sam Chumley was about to begin his first job as a delivery boy for the General Post!

Behind him the door opened.

"Pleased with yourself, young Sam?" said his grandmother with a smile. She patted his arm. "And so you should be. Mr. Trimble only chooses the best."

Mr. Albert Trimble was the head postmaster in Sam's town of Puddlewick. He was a tall, bewhiskered gentleman who wore gold spectacles and who had worked for the post office for over forty years.

Twenty boys had applied when Mr. Trimble advertised for a delivery boy. Sam remembered standing in the queue, his stomach churning with nerves. Never for a moment did he think Mr. Trimble would choose him. After he had recited his alphabet and times tables, Mr. Trimble asked him why he had applied.

All Sam could say was that he had wanted to work for the Post Office ever since he was little. Which didn't sound like a very grown-up reason.

So when Mr. Trimble announced his decision ... well! Sam had nearly fainted!

Six chimes sounded in the front hall. Sam picked up his cap. It was time to go.

As he turned towards the door, Old Mrs. Chumley held out her hand. Two brand new pennies lay in her palm.

"A penny for luck and a penny for your first letter, dear."

Sam grinned. "Thank you!"

Then he opened the front door and skipped down the street.

"Postboy!" A man leaned down from a large horse-drawn van. ROBERTSON'S REMOVALS was written across the side.

"Thank goodness, I saw you," said the man. "I've been driving round and round looking for 33 Exeter Road. An' my bet is you knows where I can find it."

Sam gave the man directions – 33 was

two doors down from his house.

"You can always trust a postboy," said the driver picking up his reins.

But Sam was already running down the street.

* * *

"What are you doing here, Sam Chumley?" snarled Edgar Buxton, the apprentice postal clerk. He was sitting at a small table in a back room behind the main post office.

Edgar stuffed a pile of envelopes into his jacket pocket.

"You ain't supposed to arrive before 6.30," he grumbled.

Sam stared at Edgar's sharp face. He

had carrot-coloured hair
and pale blue eyes that
were small and close
together.

"I do beg your
pardon," stuttered
Sam who was too
surprised to say
anything else. "I
thought …"

"You ain't here
to think," snapped
Edgar. "You're here to deliver letters and
do what I tells you."

Sam felt his face go red with anger.
Mr. Trimble had made no mention of his
being at Edgar Buxton's beck and call.

"I work for Mr. Trimble," said Sam in
a cold voice.

Edgar narrowed his mean-looking

eyes. He was just about to speak when the door opened.

"Ah, young Sam Chumley!" Mr. Trimble pulled out his waistcoat watch. "Early, too! Excellent!" He opened the heavy wooden door into the post office.

A long polished wooden counter stretched the width of the room. Two shiny sets of brass scales sat at either end. Behind the counter, a rack of empty pigeon-holes stood waiting to be filled with letters.

Sam felt excitement fizz in his stomach. He was part of the great machine called the Post Office!

"I'll show young Sam the ropes, Edgar," said Mr. Trimble as he hung up his hat and coat. "You make a start with the letters."

Edgar slowly dragged out a sack bulging with envelopes and began sorting them by letter into the pigeonholes. For a moment Sam wondered about the envelopes he had seen Edgar stuff into his pockets, but then the thought went out of his mind. For all he knew it was nothing out of the ordinary. Besides Mr. Trimble was telling him his duties and he didn't want to miss a single word!

16

2

A Girl Called Maisie

Halfway through the morning, when the coffee-and tea-rooms on the High Street were full, Sam had almost finished his first delivery.

He dragged his little red cart into a quiet road and stopped two doors up from

his own house. The letter in his hand said
Miss Maisie Summerhill, 33 Exeter
Street, Puddlewick.

Sam frowned. He
had never heard
of anyone called
Summerhill
living on
his street.
Then he
remembered
the removal van.
These Summerhills
must be the new
neighbours.

Sam walked up the path and knocked
on the front door. Almost immediately a
grey-faced maid stood in front of him.

"Postboy!" said Sam for the hundredth
time that morning.

But before the maid could take his letter, a young girl pushed past and grabbed it.

"At last!" cried Maisie Summerhill. She fixed her glossy brown eyes on Sam's face. "Do you know, Betty said she'd write every day and this is the first letter I've received."

She shook her head and her ringlets bounced on her shoulders.

"There should have been a pile of them waiting for me."

"Shh! Miss Maisie," said the maid in a stern voice. "You mustn't talk to strangers like that. What would your mother say?"

"He's not a stranger," cried Maisie. "He's the postboy."

Sam smiled despite himself.

"And I live two doors away," he said.

The maid, whose name was Nance Morgan, sniffed.

"Maybe you do, young man," she said.

"But Mrs. Summerhill ain't left her card with your mother, yet."

The door began to close. But not before Maisie Summerhill stuck her head round the side and mouthed the words 'thank you'.

As he delivered the last of his letters, Sam couldn't stop thinking of Maisie Summerhill. Usually he didn't remember much about what anyone looked like but this time he could picture Maisie's glossy brown eyes, her cheeky smile – even the dress she was wearing! Sam felt his cheeks burn. Maisie Summerhill was the prettiest girl in the world.

The next thing he knew, Sam was standing at the back of the Post Office.

In the main room Mr. Trimble and Edgar were hunched over their work. They didn't notice Sam standing at the door breathing in the aroma of ink and brown paper. To Sam it was the most beautiful smell in the world.

Mr. Trimble looked up.

"Ah, Sam. Good. Cut out these stamps please." He held up a sheet of penny black stamps and the pair of scissors that were

kept were chained to the counter.

As Sam began neatly to clip out the stamps, he could feel Mr. Trimble staring at him.

"Am I doing something wrong?" he asked nervously.

Edgar sniggered but didn't look up.

"No, no," replied Mr. Trimble quickly. He picked up his coat and hat from the stand by the door.

"I have an urgent appointment, Edgar," he said. "Would you count the letters in the pigeon holes while I'm away."

As the front door closed, an air of

menace filled the room.

"I ain't doing no dogsbody jobs like counting," muttered Edgar, who seemed to be doodling shapes in different-coloured inks. He stared at Sam. "You count 'em. You can count, can't ya?"

Sam flushed.

"Of course I can count."

"Then get on with it," said Edgar "Or I'll say you're a slacker."

Sam didn't like Edgar Buxton one bit.

But he was determined not to get into any kind of trouble with Mr. Trimble.

He put down the scissors and began counting the letters in the pigeon holes.

Sam had reached four hundred and eighty-two when he found himself staring at the name that had been floating through his mind all morning. Maisie Summerhill.

It was the same handwriting as on the letter he had delivered that morning. Sam felt his heart beat a little faster. That meant Maisie would be pleased to see him. That is if she was at home for the afternoon delivery.

"What you stopped counting for," growled Edgar. "Mr. Trimble will be back soon." He made a nasty face. "And we wouldn't want to keep him waiting, would we?"

Two minutes later, Sam put the last letter back in the XYZ hole. It was for Mr. Yardley, the butcher.

"Five hundred and thirty-four," said Sam.

At that moment, the door opened.

"Five hundred and thirty-four, sir!" said Edgar smartly as Mr. Trimble walked into the room.

Mr. Trimble stopped dead.

"Are you sure, Edgar?"

"Quite sure, sir."

The door opened again.

"What's the matter with you, Albert Trimble," cried an old lady in a black bonnet. "Are

you going to stand like a statue or will you sell me stamp?"

"I'm sorry, Mrs. Montgomery," stuttered Mr. Trimble. "Edgar!"

Sam took Mr. Trimble's hat and coat and hung them on the stand. The older man was white and shaking.

"Is something the matter, Mr. Trimble?" whispered Sam.

Mr. Trimble sat down behind the counter and put his head in his hands.

"I just can't understand it, Sam," he replied. "The numbers don't add up."

"I beg your pardon," said Sam.

"There are more stamped envelopes than we have sold stamps." Mr. Trimble shook his head. "It's almost as if the stamps are being re-used."

Mr. Trimble held up the rubber stamp

that printed a Maltese-shaped cross over each penny black stamp.

"But how? This red ink is permanent."

3

Trouble at the Post Office!

Sam's head was such a jumble of thoughts, he barely noticed the Cornish pasty his mother had made for his lunch.

One part of him was busy practising what he would say (without blushing) to Maisie Summerhill if she came to the door. The other part was worrying about the mystery of the stamps.

At two o'clock Sam filled his cart with the afternoon delivery and set off down the High Street. He was just about to stop at Mr. Yardley's shop, when he decided to have a quick look at Maisie's letter.

Sam shuffled through the packets and envelopes. Maisie Summerhill's letter wasn't there!

"You look as if you've swallowed a

pebble, Sam Chumley," said Ian Riddell, the butcher boy at Mr. Yardley's shop. "I'd recommend you try a pound of our best pork sausages."

Sam tried to smile. "Sorry, Ian." He held out Mr. Yardley's letter. "It's just …"

Then he had an idea. He could leave his cart behind Mr. Yardley's counter and run back to the Post Office. Maisie's letter must have fallen on the floor.

"Is Mr. Yardley about, Ian?"

Ian grinned. "No, he ain't. 'E's havin'

'is teeth pulled this afternoon."

"Could I leave my cart behind the counter for five minutes?"

Ian nodded and pushed the cart behind the counter.

"I wanted to be a post boy, too," he said. "Mr. Trimble told me to come back when my times table is in 'ere." Ian tapped his head.

"I hope you will one day," replied Sam kindly. "It would be fun to work with you."

Ian lowered his voice. "I 'eard Mrs. Montgomery talking to Mrs. Chandler about that Edgar Buxton."

Sam's ears pricked up. "What did she say?"

Ian folded his arms. "That he's a bad egg and Mr. Trimble only took him on because his brother-in-law ain't doing so well with his brick-making company and owes money to Buxton's uncle."

"I don't understand."

Ian rolled his eyes. "Buxton's uncle says, 'I'll give you longer to pay if Mr. Trimble gives Edgar a job in the Post Office.'"

"Oh." Sam felt his heart sink. "So that's why he's there."

"And 'e was thrown out of his last job," said Ian. He looked up at the shop clock. "'Ere you'd better get a move on."

The short cut to the Post Office was the next turning on the left. It was a dark narrow alley called Gossips Row.

Sam was halfway down when he saw something that made him stop dead and hide in a doorway.

At the end of the alley, where the shadows were darkest, Edgar Buxton stood talking to a street trader called Dick Widgin. Not may people talked to Dick Widgin because they said he was a thief.

Sam stuck his head out as far as he dared. He couldn't hear what

they were saying but he could see they
were haggling over some kind of deal.
Then to Sam's amazement, Dick reached
for his purse and counted out a
handful of coins.

Sam stepped back into
the shadows and felt his
heart thump in his chest.
What would Edgar
Buxton have to sell
to Dick Widgin?

Sam turned and
ran back down the
High Street.

That evening,
Sam couldn't eat the sausages his
mother had bought for his tea. He didn't
feel much like talking either. What he had
seen in the alley weighed on his mind
like a lump of lead.

"Eat up Sam, they're Mr. Yardley's best sausages," said his mother in a hurt voice.

"I'd say the lad's tired, Gwen," said Old Mrs. Chumley. She was sitting by the coal fire working on a tapestry cover for a new cushion.

It was a picture of the Queen's head as seen on a penny black stamp. It was especially for Sam.

"I'd say a hot chocolate would be best for a weary boy."

Twenty minutes later Sam swallowed the last of his chocolate and finished telling his grandmother everything that had happened that day.

Old Mrs. Chumley looked up from her cushion. "They say Dick Widgin is selling stamps," she said.

For a moment, all that could be heard

in the room was the steady ticking of the grandfather clock.

"That's impossible," said Sam. "You can only buy stamps from the Post Office."

Suddenly he almost burst into tears.

"I know Edgar Buxton is up to something," cried Sam. "I want to warn Mr. Trimble but what can I say?"

His grandmother stood up and put her hand on his arm.

"You get a good night's sleep," she said gently. "I've an idea or two and we'll talk tomorrow."

4

Grandma to the Rescue

As soon as Sam walked into the parlour
the next evening, he knew his grandmother
had something important to tell him.

"Did you have a good day, dear,"
she asked Sam as she put down her
tapestry cushion.

Sam nodded and flopped down on to a chair.

"Mr. Trimble showed me how to sort the letters into their districts," replied Sam. "He said I might work on the counter one day."

At that moment his mother came into the room. Her face was bright and happy.

"I've just called on our new neighbours," she said as she untied her bonnet. "The Summerhills."

"Did you approve of them, mother," asked Sam carefully. Sam knew that if his parents and Maisie's parents did not like

the same things, they would never meet.
Which meant he would never meet Maisie.

"Quite delightful," replied Mrs. Chumley.
"I have asked them all to come to tea
on Saturday."

Mrs. Chumley
looked at her
watch and opened
the door.

"Gracious! Is
that the time?
Tea in fifteen
minutes, Sam."

As the door closed,
Old Mrs. Chumley reached into her
needlework basket and
took out a letter and a small bottle of
stain remover.

"Now watch carefully, Sam."

Old Mrs. Chumley poured the liquid onto

a cloth. Then she laid the
envelope flat on her
table and rubbed
gently over the penny
black stamp.

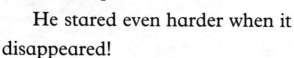

Sam stared
at the familiar
inky Maltese
cross that was
the official Post
Office stamp.

He stared even harder when it
disappeared!

Old Mrs. Chumley carefully peeled off
the wet stamp. It looked as good as new.
"How much do think Dick Widgin would
pay Edgar Buxton for this?"

Sam's mouth made a big O.

"Edgar Buxton has been stealing
posted letters for their stamps," he said in

a choked voice.

He thought of Maisie's missing letter. There must be hundreds like them. What had Edgar Buxton done with then all?

"Even if we know what Edgar Buxton is up to, we have no proof."

"Not yet," said Old Mrs. Chumley, her eyes gleaming. "But this time tomorrow, we'll have all the proof we need."

Which was why, late the following

afternoon, Sam was hiding behind a bush as his grandmother spoke to Dick Widgin.

" . . . and some of your fine black cotton, Dick," said Old Mrs Chumley. "I've a special cushion to finish before Saturday."

"Very good, Mrs. Chumley," replied Dick Widgin in his oily voice. There was a rustle of brown paper and the clip of scissors through string. "Is there anything else for you. I've some fancy velvet ribbon."

"Only a sixpence worth of penny blacks," said Old Mrs. Chumley lightly.

Hidden behind the bush, Sam swallowed hard. This was the

moment when the plan would succeed
or fail. If Dick Widgin said he had no
stamps, it would be almost impossible
to get the proof they needed.

Sam sent up a little prayer. Then he
watched as in slow motion Dick Widgin
took out a greasy pocket book from the
bottom of his tray and counted out six
penny black stamps.

"That'll be four shillings
and ten pence all in,"
he said. "If you're
sure you don't want
the ribbon."

"Quite sure,"
replied Old Mrs.
Chumley. "Sam!"

Sam jumped
out from behind
the hedge and

found himself staring straight into Dick Widgin's greasy face.

"'Ere!" cried the street trader. "What's all this about?" He looked nervously at Sam's uniform. "I ain't done nothing."

"Tell Mr. Widgin what you saw in Gossip's Alley, Sam," said Old Mrs. Chumley sternly.

Suddenly Dick Widgin looked like a hunted rabbit.

"It were his idea, not mine," he cried.

"We're quite sure the idea was Edgar Buxton's, Mr. Widgin," said Old Mrs. Chumley coldly. She handed him a piece of paper. "This letter says you admit to giving Edgar Buxton money in exchange for stamps. Sign it and you are free to leave the area."

"What if I don't," muttered Dick Widgin.

Old Mrs. Chumley pressed her lips together.

"Then the constable will hear of it

immediately."

The moment Dick Widgin made his mark, Old Mrs. Chumley handed Sam another letter marked 'Edgar Buxton By Hand'.

"Take this to Mrs. Beamish's lodging house on Maple Street," she said. "Hurry now. There's no time lose."

5

All's Well That Ends Well

When Sam arrived at the Post Office early the next morning at the back entrance, he couldn't believe his eyes.

A big pile of envelopes had been dumped outside the back door. Sam reached down and pulled one out. The inky cross was rubbed away and the stamp had been removed!

Sam pulled out another and another. They were all the same. These were the letters that Edgar Buxton had stolen!

He found a sack and began to stuff the envelopes into it before they blew away.

"Sam, the Post Office has been deceived. Edgar Buxton . . . " Mr. Trimble stood at the post office door. His face was

grey and his shoulders
drooped. When he
bent down to help pick
up the letters he was
shaking so much he kept
dropping them.

"I know about all
Edgar Buxton, sir,"
replied Sam quietly.
He stuffed the last of
the envelopes into the
sack and carried them
into the main room.

"Of course, you do."
Mr. Trimble shook his
head as if he was trying to clear his
thoughts. "Your grandmother wrote.
I am indebted to you both." His voice
trailed away.

Sam looked up at the clock. It was

almost seven. The morning delivery would be late.

Quietly and quickly, as if he had done the same thing every day for years, Sam set out the scales, the sheet of penny black stamps and the glue. Then he emptied the stolen envelopes onto the counter.

"Don't worry, Mr. Trimble. I know what to do."

Mr. Trimble smiled a small sad smile. "Yes, Sam" he said. "I believe you do."

For twenty minutes the two of them worked side by side.

Finally, Mr. Trimble cleared his throat.

"I made a terrible mistake with Edgar Buxton, Sam," he said slowly. "I will not make a mistake this time." He paused and fixed Sam with his tired grey eyes. "Will you be my apprentice clerk?"

Sam couldn't believe his ears.

"What? I mean, yes I ..."

At that moment, the door opened and Ian Riddell rushed into the room.

"Mr. Trimble!" sir," he cried. "My times tables!" Ian tapped his head. "They're in 'ere, sir, just like you wanted."

Mr. Trimble stood up and looked at both boys. His eyes were clear and his face wasn't saggy anymore.

"Gracious me!" he said. "I declare I have a new clerk and a new delivery boy in one morning!"

Ian's face went bright red.

"You mean I have the job?"

"You certainly do, Ian!"

Sam looked at Ian and both of them let out a great whoop of delight.

"Heavens!" cried Mr. Trimble, taking off his spectacles and peering at them both. "What an extraordinary noise!"

Sam blushed and stared at his hands. Which was when he saw the letter with Maisie Summerhill's name on it. He felt the two penny coins in his pocket. What had his grandmother said? One for luck and one for your first letter.

It was Friday February 13. Saturday was Valentine's Day.

Sam knew exactly who his first letter would be sent to!

"Excuse me, Mr. Trimble," he said, nervously. "May I make an errand. I'll only be five minutes."

"An extraordinary request, Sam," replied Mr. Trimble. Then he smiled. "But it's an extraordinary day. Off you go. I shall start showing Ian his duties."

Five minutes later Sam returned with a pink card in a pink envelope carefully hidden in his jacket. He put his last penny into the cash box, cut out a penny black stamp and glued it on to the envelope.

Then he slipped the letter into the pigeon hole marked S.

"What's up?" said Ian, coming into the room with the red cart. "You look like the cat that got the cream."

Sam stared at the post office around him. He saw the long gleaming counter, the shiny scales. He smelt the smell of ink and brown paper. It was the loveliest smell in the world.

In his mind's eye, he could clearly picture Maisie Summerhill. She was the loveliest girl in the world and she was coming to tea at his house this Saturday, on St. Valentine's Day.

Sam felt a huge smile stretch across his face.

"I am the cat that got the cream, Ian," he cried. "I'm the happiest, luckiest boy in the world."

Notes

The Penny Post

The Penny Post was founded by
Rowland Hill and began in 1840.
Before that the cost of posting a
letter varied from town to town
and county to county. Also
people paid when they
received a letter, not when
they posted one.

The Maltese Cross

Hand stamps were given to
postmasters for 'cancelling' the postage
stamps. In this way, it was obvious when a
stamp had been used.
They were in the
shape of a Maltese
cross. Over the years,
these handstamps
were lost and new
ones made. The
crosses often varied
from the original.

The Penny Black

A competition was held to the design this stamp. The Queen's head was chosen because it was familiar. The problem was that the ink on the black stamp was more permanent than the red ink of the 'Maltese cross'. This allowed people to rub off the ink and re-use the stamp. After only nine months, the penny black was replaced by the penny red which could not be re-used.

New Neighbours

In Victorian times, there were strict social rules about getting to know new neighbours. Ladies left visiting cards at each other's houses. This was a signal that a return visit would be welcomed. No visits could be made unless a card was received and exchanged.

Daily Deliveries

There were many
more daily postal
deliveries in
Victorian times
than there are
now. Post was
carried in hands
carts, five-wheeled
pedal cycles and
special mail coaches.

Happy Valentine's Day!

Cards, especially Valentines,
became hugely popular
when the penny post
began. The Victorians
loved sending fancy
Valentines decorated
with satin and lace.
Before the post, people
had to leave their
valentines at their
sweetheart's door. Receiving
them through the post was
much more exciting!

Sparks: Historical Adventures

ANCIENT GREECE
The Great Horse of Troy – The Trojan War
0 7496 3369 7 (hbk)   0 7496 3538 X (pbk)
The Winner's Wreath – Ancient Greek Olympics
0 7496 3368 9 (hbk)   0 7496 3555 X (pbk)

INVADERS AND SETTLERS
Viking Raiders – A Norse Attack
0 7496 3089 2 (hbk)   0 7496 3457 X (pbk)
Boudica Strikes Back – The Romans in Britain
0 7496 3366 2 (hbk)   0 7496 3546 0 (pbk)
Erik's New Home – A Viking Town
0 7496 3367 0 (hbk)   0 7496 3552 5 (pbk)
TALES OF THE ROWDY ROMANS
The Great Necklace Hunt
0 7496 2221 0 (hbk)   0 7496 2628 3 (pbk)
The Lost Legionary
0 7496 2222 9 (hbk)   0 7496 2629 1 (pbk)
The Guard Dog Geese
0 7496 2331 4 (hbk)   0 7496 2630 5 (pbk)
A Runaway Donkey
0 7496 2332 2 (hbk)   0 7496 2631 3 (pbk)

TUDORS AND STUARTS
Captain Drake's Orders – The Armada
0 7496 2556 2 (hbk)   0 7496 3121 X (pbk)
London's Burning – The Great Fire of London
0 7496 2557 0 (hbk)   0 7496 3122 8 (pbk)
Mystery at the Globe – Shakespeare's Theatre
0 7496 3096 5 (hbk)   0 7496 3449 9 (pbk)
Stranger in the Glen – Rob Roy
0 7496 2586 4 (hbk)   0 7496 3123 6 (pbk)
A Dream of Danger – The Massacre of Glencoe
0 7496 2587 2 (hbk)   0 7496 3124 4 (pbk)
A Queen's Promise – Mary Queen of Scots
0 7496 2589 9 (hbk)   0 7496 3125 2 (pbk)
Over the Sea to Skye – Bonnie Prince Charlie
0 7496 2588 0 (hbk)   0 7496 3126 0 (pbk)
Plague! – A Tudor Epidemic
0 7496 3365 4 (hbk)   0 7496 3556 8 (pbk)
TALES OF A TUDOR TEARAWAY
A Pig Called Henry
0 7496 2204 4 (hbk)   0 7496 2625 9 (pbk)
A Horse Called Deathblow
0 7496 2205 9 (hbk)   0 7496 2624 0 (pbk)
Dancing for Captain Drake
0 7496 2234 2 (hbk)   0 7496 2626 7 (pbk)
Birthdays are a Serious Business
0 7496 2235 0 (hbk)   0 7496 2627 5 (pbk)

VICTORIAN ERA
The Runaway Slave – The British Slave Trade
0 7496 3093 0 (hbk)   0 7496 3456 1 (pbk)
The Sewer Sleuth – Victorian Cholera
0 7496 2590 2 (hbk)   0 7496 3128 7 (pbk)
Convict! – Criminals Sent to Australia
0 7496 2591 0 (hbk)   0 7496 3129 5 (pbk)
An Indian Adventure – Victorian India
0 7496 3090 6 (hbk)   0 7496 3451 0 (pbk)
Farewell to Ireland – Emigration to America
0 7496 3094 9 (hbk)   0 7496 3448 0 (pbk)

The Great Hunger – Famine in Ireland
0 7496 3095 7 (hbk)   0 7496 3447 2 (pbk)
Fire Down the Pit – A Welsh Mining Disaster
0 7496 3091 4 (hbk)   0 7496 3450 2 (pbk)
Tunnel Rescue – The Great Western Railway
0 7496 3353 0 (hbk)   0 7496 3537 1 (pbk)
Kidnap on the Canal – Victorian Waterways
0 7496 3352 2 (hbk)   0 7496 3540 1 (pbk)
Dr. Barnardo's Boys – Victorian Charity
0 7496 3358 1 (hbk)   0 7496 3541 X (pbk)
The Iron Ship – Brunel's Great Britain
0 7496 3355 7 (hbk)   0 7496 3543 6 (pbk)
Bodies for Sale – Victorian Tomb-Robbers
0 7496 3364 6 (hbk)   0 7496 3539 8 (pbk)
Penny Post Boy – The Victorian Postal Service
0 7496 3362 X (hbk)   0 7496 3544 4 (pbk)
The Canal Diggers – The Manchester Ship Canal
0 7496 3356 5 (hbk)   0 7496 3545 2 (pbk)
The Tay Bridge Tragedy – A Victorian Disaster
0 7496 3354 9 (hbk)   0 7496 3547 9 (pbk)
Stop, Thief! – The Victorian Police
0 7496 3359 X (hbk)   0 7496 3548 7 (pbk)
Miss Buss and Miss Beale – Victorian Schools
0 7496 3360 3 (hbk)   0 7496 3549 5 (pbk)
Chimney Charlie – Victorian Chimney Sweeps
0 7496 3351 4 (hbk)   0 7496 3551 7 (pbk)
Down the Drain – Victorian Sewers
0 7496 3357 3 (hbk)   0 7496 3550 9 (pbk)
The Ideal Home – A Victorian New Town
0 7496 3361 1 (hbk)   0 7496 3553 3 (pbk)
Stage Struck – Victorian Music Hall
0 7496 3367 0 (hbk)   0 7496 3554 1 (pbk)
TRAVELS OF A YOUNG VICTORIAN
The Golden Key
0 7496 2360 8 (hbk)   0 7496 2632 1 (pbk)
Poppy's Big Push
0 7496 2361 6 (hbk)   0 7496 2633 X (pbk)
Poppy's Secret
0 7496 2374 8 (hbk)   0 7496 2634 8 (pbk)
The Lost Treasure
0 7496 2375 6 (hbk)   0 7496 2635 6 (pbk)

20th-CENTURY HISTORY
Fight for the Vote – The Suffragettes
0 7496 3092 2 (hbk)   0 7496 3452 9 (pbk)
The Road to London – The Jarrow March
0 7496 2609 7 (hbk)   0 7496 3132 5 (pbk)
The Sandbag Secret – The Blitz
0 7496 2608 9 (hbk)   0 7496 3133 3 (pbk)
Sid's War – Evacuation
0 7496 3209 7 (hbk)   0 7496 3445 6 (pbk)
D-Day! – Wartime Adventure
0 7496 3208 9 (hbk)   0 7496 3446 4 (pbk)
The Prisoner – A Prisoner of War
0 7496 3212 7 (hbk)   0 7496 3455 3 (pbk)
Escape from Germany – Wartime Refugees
0 7496 3211 9 (hbk)   0 7496 3454 5 (pbk)
Flying Bombs – Wartime Bomb Disposal
0 7496 3210 0 (hbk)   0 7496 3453 7 (pbk)
12,000 Miles From Home – Sent to Australia
0 7496 3370 0 (hbk) 0 7496 3542 8 (pbk)